It's a GiRL ThiNg!

SMART, FIERCE, and LEADING THE WAY

by Pri Ferrari

🍓 StarBerry Books
New York

This book's first edition in Brazil had the support of 250 people who contributed to a crowdfunding campaign. To everyone who helped, for every shared link, to every voice who joined this fight: my eternal gratitude.

For friends, family, and many others who share the dream of living in a more fair and egalitarian world and who have helped this project become real —Pri Ferrari

© 2016, by Pri Ferrari
First published in Brazil by Companhia das Letras, São Paulo
English translation rights arranged through S.B.Rights Agency – Stephanie Barrouillet
Translation copyright © 2019 by Kane Press, Inc.

Publisher's Cataloging-in-Publication data

Names: Ferrari, Pri, author.
Title: It's a girl thing!: Smart, fierce, and leading the way / by Pri Ferrari.
Description: New York, NY: StarBerry Books, an imprint of Kane Press, Inc., 2019.
Summary: An exploration of who girls are and what they can be.
Identifiers: ISBN 9781635921243 (Hardcover) | 9781635921250 (ebook) | LCCN 2018954719
Subjects: LCSH: Women--Employment--Juvenile literature. | Women--Vocational guidance--Juvenile literature. | Occupations--Juvenile literature. | Self-esteem in children--Juvenile literature. | Self-esteem in adolescence--Juvenile literature. | CYAC: Women--Employment. | Women--Vocational guidance. | Occupations. | Self-esteem in children. | Self-esteem in adolescence. | BISAC: JUVENILE NONFICTION / Girls & Women | JUVENILE NONFICTION / Careers | JUVENILE NONFICTION / Social Topics / Self-Esteem & Self-Reliance
Classification: LCC HD6095 .F47 2019 | DDC 331.4/024/055--dc23

10 9 8 7 6 5 4 3 2 1

First published in the United States of America in 2019 by StarBerry Books, an imprint of Kane Press, Inc.
Printed in China

StarBerry Books is a registered trademark of Kane Press, Inc.

Book Design: Michelle Martinez

Visit us online at www.kanepress.com

 Like us on Facebook
k.com/kanepress

 Follow us on Twitter
@KanePress

What do girls like to do?

What can girls BE?

Girls are

PILOTS.

They can fly helicopters, airplanes, rockets . . . and even dragons.

Girls are

ARCHEOLOGISTS.

They dig up bones and explore ancient cities.
They learn about all the people and
creatures that have lived on Earth.

Girls are

They play soccer and basketball
and football. They swim and surf
and become fast and strong.

Girls are

They cook all kinds of dishes,
from the simplest to the fanciest.

Girls are

They climb to the highest peaks in the world so they can touch the clouds.

Girls are

DOCTORS.

They operate on patients and
make sick people feel better.

Girls are

They rocket into space and make amazing discoveries about our universe.

Girls are

They draw and paint. They invent stories
about wizards and aliens and superheroes.

Girls are

MUSICIANS.

They sing and dance. They play
all kinds of instruments, from
violins to electric guitars.

Girls are

MECHANICS.

They fix cars and trucks and
motorcycles. They hit the road
and travel all over the world.

Girls are

They explore worlds, escape
from magical mazes, and beat
the hardest levels.

Girls are

They have stellar ideas, lead huge teams
of workers, and run amazing companies.

Girls are

CHEMISTS.

They work with solids, liquids, and gases. They make mixtures and creations that change the world.

Girls are

ADVENTURERS.

They dive down deep into the ocean to see
strange and wonderful creatures.

Girls are

ARCHITECTS.

They design parks, museums, houses,
and skyscrapers.

Girls are

BUS DRIVERS.

They love to be part of their community and help people get where they need to be.

Girls are

They take risks daily to put
out fires and save lives.

Girls are

They fight fearlessly against the
toughest monsters you can imagine!

Girls are

POWERFUL.

Their work is important. They are judges, senators, mayors, queens, and presidents.

So what do girls like?
And what can they be?

Anything in the world!

A Girl Thing is

EVERYTHING!

ABOUT THE AUTHOR

Pri Ferrari is the author and illustrator of *It's a Girl Thing!: Smart, Fierce, and Leading the Way,* her first children's book.

She resides in São Paulo, Brazil.

She believes the world can be a better place and is ready to help make change!